Also by Beatrice Hawley

Making the House Fall Down
alicejamesbooks (1977)

nothing is lost

by beatrice hawley

Apple-wood Press   Cambridge   1979

ACKNOWLEDGMENTS

For permission to reprint some of these poems, the author wishes to thank the editors of the following: Aspect, Greenhouse, The Real Paper, Zeugma.

ISBN: 0-918222-05-2 hardcover
ISBN: 0-918222-06-0 paperback

nothing is
lost

For
John Reynolds Burkhardt
&
Rebecca Sweet Burkhardt
&
Sarah Hawley Fink

CONTENTS

ZHENIA

Once when I had bribed the guard
with my last sweater
I was allowed to spend one week
in the long shed
washing dishes.

When the supervisor noticed
that I enjoyed the warmth
from the sink full of water,
I was sent out to serve
the thin cabbage broth
which was the main meal.

A transport of men from the mines
arrived.
Before me stood a bundle of rags
with a gaping hole for a mouth:
"Look, a woman!"
Something posessed me
and I leaned over the table
and kissed him,
full on his bleeding lips.

BARBARA'S POEM

for Barbara Nielsen Whitcomb on the occasion of her ordination as Deacon
of the Episcopal Church; and for Barbara, martyr, 6th Century

Your day comes on me
too soon each year
I am not ready.

In your garden
the plants were like jewels, Barbara,
I can still see your hands etched against green;
I miss you.

Why so foolish, Barbara?
You could have stayed safe inside,
sherberts and ice brought in;
you could have spent your life with carpets,
cushions, small boxes of candy, me.

You let the strangers in.
Willful, spoiled, rich man's daughter
indulging yourself with scholars;
at night the lamps burned in the tower.

Jewel of your father's eye:
was it his looks? That simple one
you let come in, finally, alone?
Plain cheese I called him, and you laughed.

Later, I remember you heaving treasures
out the window,
garnishing the corridors with plain wood crosses:
I could have told you where that would end.

A rich girl's fancy: austerity—
and what else I will not mention.

Did you need the third window
so all the world could see through you?
The day you had it built
I said goodbye to you in my mind.

Barbara, I miss you.

I don't think of that day.
Your father, screaming, pulling you by the hair
down to the city
the fire.

The place is empty.
No one is left now
without you these gardens are haunted.
I am alone.
All day I wander about saying: *Barbara,
Barbara, where are you?*

My rough hands tear the silks you left
crumpled in a corner.
For the sake of a window, foolish one,
for an invisible nothing called soul.

KATHRYN PICCARD

In the town where I grew up
the trees met overhead, making
a tunnel of grecn to walk under.
Among us divorce was unheard of;
when my parents did it
I could not see.
That is, I went blind
or partly
or in panic
or faked it. I couldn't see.

There is always one child
who gets teased.

The one thing we did every week
was to go to church Sundays—
I was just a child there
among the other children.
I liked the music and didn't
mind the grown-ups not letting
the children have doughnuts.

And camp, and girl scouts, I loved that.
It was fine. I could
always do that
even when I was blind.

Then I was confirmed. In church,
in Christ's church. Though I took longer
deciding than the others:
it was a matter of finally getting hungry,
needing food that was more than food.

It is not easy to drift into this world.
I had to push my way in,
my white hands clenched.

2

My grandmother flew in a balloon
before I was born.
And I did once, my knee frozen,
the little town below too far:
if you aren't afraid of heights
it is dangerous to be a balloonist.

Now she and I are both priests.
Women priests, two-headed calves,
looking together at twice as many stars.
I am her safeguard on the icy streets,
she is frail, I am as big as she,
she is changing, she is still hurting,
she still wants her sisters to come back.

People don't always choose everything.
I have simply rooted where I was planted.

I am growing here quite well.

I am cracking my share of stones
in this church, in a hundred years
no one will understand
what all this fuss is about.

Maybe we are all stupid together:
all I am doing
is what seems obvious and clear
as bells, ringing to greet us in,
me and gramdma.

holding each other's hands
as we slide together
straight into church and
right to the very front with
wine with bread.

JOAN OF ARC

"For the most part I do the thing which my own nature drives me to do"
—*Albert Einstein*

1

In these green hills
my brother and I run fast.
St. Margaret speaks to me here.
Her face is clean,
I call her light.
She tells me I am chosen
and I know the reason:
strong legs
a sound belly
and straight teeth.

2

I steal my cousin's clothes,
I cut my hair,
I run far.
No one knows me.

3

I must not look back.
But I miss Hauviette most.
In bed at night we played
lovers.
I didn't say goodbye
because I missed her
even before I left.

Before I return she will be fat, she will have
    children.

4

I had a red dress
I will never wear again.
A rich man gives me
a horse, armour, men.

Staying a virgin
turns out to be easy;
I am ugly and healthy.
The silly king himself
hates my peasant breath:
garlic is a useful plant.
In the fields at night
curled up with soldiers,
I reek.

5

After I annoint him
with King David's oil
which is so old and hard
I have to use a gold needle
and prick his forehead,
he goes to sleep.

I eat no meat
take baths, am visited by strange ladies who are
    not interesting.
I have not seen St. Catherine for weeks.

The king plays games in his garden,
and won't fight.

I wear my suit of armour
every day.
My red dress is gone
and I do not want another.

6

Is he a bastard after all?

7

It seems the English at least
take me seriously.
This little round room
is a prison.
But I can see trees.
Sometimes a person can't help
thinking
about her home and her friend.

When I jumped from the tower
I held on, in my mind,
to the corner of my mother's kitchen
where I used to peel vegetables
and so was not hurt.

8

Nothing lasts.
They told me to save France,
so I did.

They didn't tell me
the time would be so short,
so many days spent
sitting in the king's garden.

9

Tomorrow in the flames
I will think of riding my horse,
which was the best of all

and I will
be called brave.

FLOWER CHILD

for Linda Kasabian

1

I've put my beads away
and can't remember where
in Death Valley I buried
my box of feathers.

2

You've heard of living
outside the body?
A stranger in the bus station
describes flying over red stones
so you follow that stranger
home like a dog.

3

Anything is possible.
If people do it, it's human.
We were only try ing to live forever
like anyone else.

4

If I had been allowed,
that night, to join the others
I would have crossed over
and learned what they know
and won't tell.

But I was on the lawn.

5

So I tell
the story over and over,
my face never stops being pale
I never stop shaking
I hope when I am dead
I will forget
the terrible face of my lover.

BOUDICCA

"Now she grasped a spear, to strike fear in all who watched her "—Deo Cassius

Hair is a flame,
visible for miles.
A tall woman
carries a shield as tall as she.

This is a cold country.
For many days the blades of grass
are sharp, in the wood houses
winter keeps the people in one place.

Hours of telling
and telling again. Hair,
even hers, singed by the fire
as we lean towards the bright faces.

Hours of telling and telling again,
all the world's known things
carried in our mouths:
the queen in winter takes fire
into her body,
in the field blazes.

IL MARCHESE

1942

The pilots came and lifted me
beyond the wishes my mother had for my life.

They fell in my field,
I found them in a tangle of string,
wide-eyed:
England.

We buried the evidence.
Two of us carried the third
between us and even his bleeding
lost itself among my grain.
I hid them for three years.
We played bridge.

When it was over my boys went home.

Mother is dead,
the house too big.
I ache when I walk too far.

1950

The Americans have come here
because of the garden,
and for the sake of the health of their children.

The neighbour, Il Marchese
comes for tea.

They find him quaint and marvelous;
kind to the children.

His love of animals
has made him gentle.

He points out nests, snails, ant hills.
He teaches the children:
"Leave a bowl of milk on the steps
and you will see a hedgehog."

1969

"I've come back to see you, Valdemar,
look, I'm a woman,
here is my little boy:
we've come to see the garden."

On the way to a restaurant
you make the taxi stop in the park
at the center of the city.

You open a large wicker basket
full of rats:
"They like the city best" you say.

Out of love
I do not scream.

DOMINA

for Sylvia Plath

A woman walks in a small section
of the world.
She carries something sharp:
her hands are bleeding
and the sun beats through
slivers of glass, setting fires.

For the broken glass
you carry, I forgive you.
Though in trying to get rid of it
you have pushed in deep
into the hearts of people
who would have shown you light
without hurting your eyes.

We who would love you burn;
you are made not to see us
and in our generation
we have lost the trick
of knowing how to feed
those who never die.

You are among us so close;
and here we are, arms fill of roses
we're ready to give you,
and milk, and a blue bowl—
if you would only look.

Put yourself among clouds, then;
there is your bed
there is your blanket
you can look at us in safety
we cradle, we rock you to sleep.

A woman walks between two sections
of a small city
in such confusion:
takes light into her own hands
and is forgiven, even by strangers.

LETTER FROM
THE COLONIES

I have not known such cold, sister,
we are locked in each other's arms
for weeks here, the ground is iron.

There is a certain loveliness:
you should see the sun on ice,
though our eyes ache looking.

We will stay. There have been not a few
deaths and the ground is too hard for graves;
but we will stay. There is some food.

The savages have tamed the ground
enough for that, we profit and learn;
we are as angels beside them.

I am certain you should come—
a few winters away we will have made
dominion of every thing we see.

ANGELS

God's messengers on earth
are terrible and those who look
at their faces become blind and go crazy.

They are light-as-razor, light
as that-which-burns they are not visible.

A coal burning in the mouth
is like an angel, and at night
they steal the children who die.

People have walked, bandaged
for miles in the desert
after speaking with only one angel.

Good angels are more like fire;
harder than bad angels
and more dangerous.

Bad angels are only angels
who live in dark places
blind and trapped.

No one has seen an angel for years.
They are away, dancing and not dancing.

NEIGHBOUR

I worry about her.
She seems so nervous about the children,
never letting them out of her sight.
She has a new baby but has grown so thin
she's lost all her milk.

In the blizzard, the only time
we ever spoke, I frightened her.
She wouldn't take milk from me,
even for the baby, who was crying.
The husband walked for miles in the storm
to get the milk. He wouldn't speak at all.

I believe she's crazy, as much as she
believes I am. I wonder if she watches
when I take my clothes off at night.

Or maybe the husband watches the woman next
    door
getting undressed and his wife knows,
which makes her unable to eat solid food, which
    drives her crazy.

PRISON VISIT

for Ella Ellison

Some people know how to wait.
You wait,
you wait on a green bench near the trees.
You are waiting for the trees to move,
to lead you out
past the fence.

When I visit you
we lie on our backs and see
a tangle of branches against the sky.
I say they are a wonderful basket for catching fish.

You say they have caught you
and that looking at branches
without the fence behind them
stings your eyes,

that the fence at least
makes you not forget
where you are.

THREE RAVENS

I have black hair
and I saw three ravens
and I know what that means:
I'm getting out soon.

My last furlough
I got married
(only of course, not legal
it was with a woman)
Anyway, she's going to look out for me, she says.

My husband used to raise his finger to me
like I was a kid.

It was because I tried to hide the body,
they gave me such a stretch. If I had
only stabbed him and cried it wouldn't
have been so bad, my lawyer said. But
my kids are grown, they don't miss me.

My son didn't think I'm a witch
but I told him about a certain hailstorm
which he called me long distance
to say was true.

They're all scared of me,
all the people
a good woman and I say those three birds
prove it.

THE WEAVER

She doesn't move much.
The skeins are set in baskets,
spilling colors into her lap.
They glow. She chooses by setting
them side by side in the sun.

She has sky-blue,
blood-red, snail shell color,
color for under a stone,
the shade for a child's throat,
dark green of the footprint on grass.

The patterns are subtle, they change
very little. Mistakes lie in a heap,
banners fly from the window; child, root, fish, all
woven together, the dead and the living.

THE WOMAN
WHO KNITS

Her tension is even,
she is the French farm wife
(mother of an idiot savante)
who leans each day
against her white-walled house
and knits a sock
turning the heel
as the mailman turns the corner.

At night her boy sleeps
on the floor near the oven,
her husband's heart hammers
against her back.
She keeps awake,
imagines the new pattern: cast on, divide evenly—
knit two, pearl two
until sock reaches desired length,
use double-pointed steel needles.

THE SPELL
for Patricia Cumming

I want to know how you could
and stay in the world:

a woman who goes to the store
to buy apples for her daughters

comes home and puts them in a wooden bowl,
her daughters eat them,

goes up to her room
and makes spells against pain.

Trying this has made more than
one woman turn to stone,

another, for example, spends years
making her tongue say all eyes are not tricks.

LOT'S WIFE

A quiet garden:
lemon trees in pots
big as children
learning to walk
but with hands still shaped
like starfish.

A girl is climbing,
wet bark between her knees;
frogs small as flowers
swim in the pond.

If you look back
you will turn into salt.

THE BAD MOTHER

Remember that in the evening, just at supper
we would sometimes see
children burning.

You were just a baby.
I would rock you in front of the TV
your father would come home late
from his work, and sometimes
not for days.

I would rock you there and
each time they showed the dead people
or a young boy screaming
I would stiffen and you would start to cry.

Then later, when we were alone, all the time,
the walls would collapse
around me and I would have gone myself
straight into the picture and stood
with the others.
You crying in the evening had become
a pattern of living.

I was the good mother.

The bad mother left her children behind
and was on television
becoming a fanatic,
crazy: she spent two years
in prison, not eating,
while her children were home, alone, waiting
for their mother, the bad mother.

They kept
a Christmas tree standing for two years
until she came back.

SIREN

The wreath of flowers around her head
is wilting
but her eyes still burn.
She stands on a small island
and the waters are rising.
He wants to take a little boat
there and lift her in it,
row safely back to the wooden pier
where they sell taffy.
If he can get something sweet
into her mouth she may speak,
she may wrap him into her cloak,
she may be still.
But his hands are bleeding,
it's cold,
she throws rocks.

CLAIRVOYANCE

She is afraid
or a tower of strength
turning, before his eyes, to salt.

She wishes the crystal
hanging in the window
could transmit more than light.

Wise lovers know the future:
journeys, separation.

AUBADE
Even in China
it cracks us apart.
Dust is already pouring
over the children's faces
and we can see it.

The room fills with light
as we move away.
Now we are two unknown people,
putting on socks and shoes.

WATER

You wrench away from me fast
then come back to my door
with bowls of water, not milk;
not even a flower
floats on the surface.

I want no water.
In the desert the water is buried
inside eggshells. Only the people
who live there know where it's hidden
and they don't tell strangers.

Or I want all water,
an ocean floor, maybe, where no one
hides anything, where survival
means being able to grow fins.

But I'm here. It's raining.
Every cupped thing in the garden is spilling over.

AMNESIA

First, the name of your father,
then your house.

You are standing among trees
they glow, they are covered
with a veil of ice.
The ground beneath your feet
is white, you are in snow.
You wear a white dress,
you wear dancing shoes.

But you are among the trees
the heel of your dancing
shoe is broken,
you carry it in your hand.

There is blood on the hem
of your white dress.
The dress is a costume.

There are two pairs of footprints
behind you, leading back
through the trees to a white
spread of lawn.

The snow is making you blind.

One pair of footprints does not lead
as far as you have come.
Part of the way the heel
of your shoe was not broken.

Walking towards the house
you forget you were running,
you forget the color of your hair.

Closer, you forget if you are big
or small. You forget the heel
of your shoe is in your hand.

Near the door
people are gathered
they watch you stumble toward them.

They are holding blankets,
they are holding their
arms out wide to gather
you in. They are strangers.

A man wraps you in blankets
a woman smooths out your hair.
She wants to take you upstairs
to the bed and give you hot milk

she wants to know where
is your lover.

HIDE OUT

You decide to hide near a river.
You build a house of reeds,
one room, an upside down basket.

No one can find you
any more. Your shoes are worn out.

There are fish to eat from the river,
the water is clear
you can walk alone for miles, seeing
nothing but the faint marks
of your own footsteps.

You can hide out forever;
this is a place no one knows.

Though at night, hugging your own body
you can hear the otters in the distance:
barking, coming closer.

LOSS

Your diamonds are lost,
you aren't here any more:
we sold your last skirt;
seller and buyer blind to the cloth:

you aren't here any more
even the children have covered their ears
seller and buyer blind to the cloth
the gold thread is not visible

even the children have covered their ears
glass houses surround us, diamonds are for music
the gold thread is not visible
some of us think we remember the way

glass houses surround us, diamonds are for music
fish do not speak, wishes are not granted
some of us try and remember the way
water beat when you drowned, the flat sound.

REMEDIES

for Dashell Hammet

A long sea-voyage:
lean on the polished railing
in your white shawl:
spit into water.

A revolution:
learn to hide in the jungle
where people can be mistaken
for a new kind of flower

A new lover:
lie in a hammock
smoke opium together
dye your hair orange, curl it.

A shopping expedition:
in the most elegant store,
buy a red dress, a fan—
a pearl handled revolver.

LAMENT

You are farther away
than an island of black grapes
and the boat
which makes an icy crossing
as it approaches:
the church, the house, the vineyard:—
so far.

IN THE MINES

1
Another Place

Give over to the strange chairs,
the soft bed. Something
different for breakfast
or no breakfast or at a different time.

The confusing location of the new bed
windows on the wrong wall
the wrong tree.

Awake, stiff, uncertain
about where to put the dirty sheets—
to wash a cup or leave it.

Far from home, among strangers
light changes everything.

2
Leaves

Fill your mouth with berries,
stain your hands and lips
purple, come to the pond—
walk in, not looking
at where you put your feet.

You are learning
that a tangle of roots
connects the entire
round world.

3
Green Mountains

Green mountains have closed eyes.
When they awaken we will know giants again,
they will walk about
splitting open the ground.

We will live in caves again
in rooms carved by water
we will taste those fish,
the blind ones that glow.

The mountains wait only for the buzz of voices to
change.

A deeper sound will wake them,
will open the dark world.

4
Outside

You are in a world of strangers
made of glass
and they can break you.

Your face is a mask too,
you aren't the only one who sees
flames in other people's eyes.

When you buy a dress covered with roses
realize that someone with the same confusion
has gone before you, pasting them on.

Remember the lights at night
show the rooms of houses
where people live, lifting spoons
to their mouths, as you do sometimes, feeling
the warmth on their tongues.

Remember these things,
learn them: step out
and look into mirrors, into windows:
fragility is enduring.

5
Autumn Sky

Look at it.
You may be saved.
The wind comes from water.
Away from this sharp grass
a house near the ocean waits.

It is your house
if you make it.

The same sky which covers you now covers this
house.

You can go there,
even walking
one step at a time.

Before winter you can be making soup
on a clean stove with sweet
smelling walls around you.

6
In the Mines

Make no mistake, this tunneling will be a success
you will find an end.
As by putting one foot
in front of the other, following the edge of sand
you could step
in every country.

When you emerge,
fists full of hard rock,
you will own light.

In the mines it is always dark.
The treasure is not visible
but it sorrounds you.
Take it.

Remember only that it's like
digging a hole to China
on a dry, hot day
and reaching, after a long time, water.

RED BOOTS

We lived in palaces of stone
before we were born.
Leaning our arms
on the window-sills
we could see our mothers,
running, wearing red boots

TRUE LIES

Always a stranger among us:
hidden pockets in your coat—
you are ready to move
at a moment's notice.

That's the story you tell us,
flaming your hair with your long fingers.
But it's a lie.

You have no secrets in your coat,
no small tickets folded away.
Even when you cut your hair,
you stayed.

If you burn down the house
and the blackberry bushes
and let the pine trees come
you won't get away.

There are no special papers:
you are here with us, you will stay with us.
The stories you tell are only meant to scare us;
they are not necessary
we cannot abandon you.

WHERE
oak tree,
elm tree,
under the porch
out by the trash barrels
in the upstairs closet
where the blankets are

leaving small marks
until they become strange,
tall, owners of faces.

FACES

Dead people play
quiet games: push-the plants-up
and hide-the-body

so no one wants to plant
bulbs deep there.

Soon their faces melt
they are hard
to remember, like the moon,
round the invisible.

SARAH'S PLACE

Tom boy
small girl
Queen Victoria
dead, six days old:
the other children
play ball here your grave, third base.

REBECCA

"All the tired horses in the sun" —Bob Dylan

At the actual moment
of your birth, your head coming
out from between my legs,
I sang.

All through the morning of the first day
I watched.
Perfect daugher,
rose, rose, rose.

All through the morning of the first day
I watched
and saw, as afternoon came,
a shadow pass over your face.

You seemed so fierce.
Evening, night, morning,
your anger made you strong.

The evening of the second day
your face turned away.

You pushed off on some journey,
leaving behind even the moon
which came up orange that night
pulling you to another place
and a terrible new smile.

GRIEF

A grey stalk in water
sends out a flower:

nothing is lost forever.
The ones who sleep underground

come back in dreams,
wearing the faces of strangers.

We have to learn again and again
what to keep, what to throw away.

Apple-wood Press began in January 1976.
The image of the apple joined with the hard concreteness of wood in many ways expresses the goals of the press. One of the first woods used in printing, apple-wood remains a metaphor for giving ideas a form. Apple-wood Press books are published in the memory of Harry and Lillian Apple.